# Lots of Dogs

JENNIFER B. STITH

This is Don.

Don has a lot
of dots.

dot
dot
dot
dot

This is Jak.

Jak is on top of
a box.

This is Tod.

Tod has a fox.

This is Rob.

Rob is a big dog.

(Bit is not.)

Rob
Bit

This is Oz.

Oz has a pop.

pop

This is Fab.

Fab is a hog.

This is Bot.

Bot has a job.

## Phonics Focus Words: Short o

| Bot    | hog    | Oz  |
|--------|--------|-----|
| box    | job    | pop |
| dog(s) | lot(s) | Rob |
| Don    | not    | Tod |
| dot(s) | on     | top |
| fox    |        |     |

## Decodable Words

| big | Fab |
|-----|-----|
| Bit | Jak |

## High-Frequency Words

| a   | is | this |
|-----|----|------|
| has | of |      |